ELLEN GRAE

ELLEN GRAE

Vera and Bill Cleaver

Illustrated by Ellen Raskin

J · B · Lippincott

NEW YORK

ISBN 0-397-30938-4
Copyright © 1967 by Vera and William J. Cleaver
PRINTED IN THE UNITED STATES OF AMERICA
Library of Congress Catalog Card Number AC 67-10623

Typography by Tere Lo Prete

11 12 13 14 15 16 17 18 19 20

TO

SPECIAL AGENT

PHOEBE LARMORE

WITH

AFFECTION

ELLEN GRAE

Mrs. McGruder isn't a religious person especially, although she and Mr. McGruder attend the Methodist Church every Sunday and when I live with her I have to leave off being a Pantheist and turn Methodist too. But she likes to have people talk to her about religion.

So, wanting to please her, I told her that I had learned to be most truly, humbly grateful for all the benevolences God had seen fit to bestow upon me.

She turned a light green gaze upon me and asked, "Oh? What brought that on?"

"Nothing brought it on," I explained. "I just started feeling grateful toward Him. I feel grateful toward you too, Mrs. McGruder. For letting me come back down here and stay with you while I go to school. I vow that I've changed since last year and won't be as much trouble to you this year as I was last."

She said, "Well, if that's true it'll be my turn to be grateful. Like what, for instance, have you changed?"

"Well, for one thing I take a bath every night now without anybody hollering at me to do it and for another I've stopped swearing. I don't even say hell any more. I think that the use of profanity is a vocabulary deficiency, don't you?"

"At the moment I can't think," Mrs. McGruder said, handing me a freshly sugared doughnut. "I'm too busy counting my blessings."

"I know a girl whose father, they said, dropped dead from swearing. Her name's Opal Gridley. Her father's name was Fortis Alonzo and I think that's what killed him."

"I'm really trying but I don't get the connection," Mrs. McGruder said.

"You will in a minute. Well, anyway, he was a meter reader for the gas company and I guess that and his having a name like Fortis Alonzo burdened him heavily and made him feel unimportant."

"I think Fortis Alonzo is rather a pretty name," Mrs. McGruder murmured.

"Do you? Well, that's what it was. Fortis Alonzo

Gridley. He used to drive around with all the windows in his car rolled up. Even when everybody else was standing around pouring sweat and with their tongues hanging out having trouble breathing because it was so hot, Mr. Gridley would get in his car and roll up all the windows and drive around and wave to people."

"I'm still trying," Mrs. McGruder said.

"His wife was fat and could sing Italian. She practiced every night after supper. If you listened it was sadly pretty but nobody did. They'd all come out on their porches and stand around and laugh and this made Mr. Gridley mad. He'd run out of his house and shake his fist at them and swear. When he died everybody said that's what caused it. They said God struck him dead for swearing so much. But do you know something?"

"I'm beginning to think not," Mrs. McGruder said.

"Mr. Fortis Alonzo Gridley died at his own hand. Trying to make people think he was rich enough to have an air-conditioned car. He didn't have it though and that's what killed him. The heat and no air at all. I was the one who got to him first the night he collapsed. Gridley's house was next door to ours and when I saw Mr. Gridley drive up weaving and wobbling I ran over and jerked the door of his car open and he fell out. He didn't have time to say one word. Just blew a bubble and died."

"What do you mean he blew a bubble?"

"He blew a bubble while he was dying. It looked like glass. Mrs. McGruder?"

"Yes, Ellen Grae?"

"Was that telegram that came a few minutes ago from Rosemary?"

"It was from her father. She'll be in on the ten o'clock train. Are you ready for more breakfast now?"

"No thanks. I still hate breakfast; I haven't changed that much. Will I have to room with her again?"

"That's my plan. Why?"

"Oh, nothing. It's just that I was thinking it might be better if I could have a room to myself this year. I forgot to tell you and I'll bet Grace did too that lately I have these strange seizures."

"Seizures? What kind of seizures?"

"Seizures. You know. They always come at night. I get up and crash around and cry out. I know when I'm doing it but I can't stop myself. Jeff says it's a very frightening thing to watch. He says it's almost as if I was disembodied. I was just thinking it might be better if Rosemary could be spared the sight. You know how frail she is."

"No, I hadn't noticed," Mrs. McGruder said, setting two scrambled eggs and a glass of milk in front of me. "I'll be on the lookout for one of your attacks but in the meantime could you just oblige me and eat so that we can get on to more important things?"

Mrs. McGruder is a MORE person. Everything, no matter what it is, always should be MORE.

Together we went down the hall to the room that I was again to share with Rosemary and Mrs. Mc-Gruder looked at my bed and said that the sheets and spread could stand a little MORE smoothing and the pillow a little MORE plumping. Then she watched while I finished unpacking my suitcases which contained MORE books than clothes and said that I should have brought MORE dresses and that those I did bring needed MORE starch.

She looked at my white shoes and made a noise with her tongue against the roof of her mouth. "Who polished these shoes, Ellen Grae?"

"I did. Don't they look nice?"

"Yes. Except they've got MORE white on the soles than on the tops."

About ten o'clock we drove down to the village of Thicket to meet Rosemary's train but as usual it was late. Mrs. McGruder parked the car off to one side and tried to settle down to reading a magazine which she had had the foresight to bring along but couldn't because I was there.

"Goodness, Ellen Grae. Stop fidgeting."

"I'm not fidgeting. I'm itching myself. It's all those baths I've been taking. Wouldn't some boiled peanuts taste good right about now? Just to take our minds off things?"

Mrs. McGruder frowned but when she turned her head to look at me there was a gentleness in her eyes. "Oh, honey, you don't really want any boiled peanuts now, do you?"

"Some nice, salty, juicy ones. The way Ira fixes them. While we're just sitting here waiting for Rosemary I could just hop over to his stand and get us a couple of bags. I'd hurry."

Mrs. McGruder sighed but reached into her handbag and found her change purse and extracted a quarter. "All right but don't make me come after you. And watch when you cross the street."

She meant for cars, of course, but there were only three parked ones. First Street lay hot and quiet under the September sun. The only humans in sight were the clerk from Sangster's Grocery Store who was busy letting down the green window awnings, a man in white coveralls who had his head stuck in the door of the barber shop, and Ira who was setting up his stand in its customary oak-shaded spot.

A lot of people in Thicket think that Ira is crazy but he's not. He's just different. He never wears shoes even when the cold winds come sweeping down from the north, he can't read or write and he lives in a two-room tin shack down near the river bend all by himself. Mrs. McGruder told me that once upon a time Ira had a mother and father, at least a stepfather, but that one day they just picked up and left and never came back. Nobody knows how old Ira is. Mrs. McGruder says maybe thirty but I think maybe he's older because he's got white in his black hair and sometimes his dark eyes have a very old man's sadness in them. Ira lives on what money he can make selling boiled and parched peanuts and sometimes somebody patient will pay him to mow a yard. He could make a lot of money mowing yards because he's neat and careful but he won't talk to people. He just nods and points which makes everybody nervous. Even when he goes into a store to buy something that's all he does. Mrs. McGruder told me that in all the years she's been seeing Ira around town she's never heard him speak. I reckon nobody has except me. He talks to me all the time.

I skipped up to his stand and whacked the board that was his counter and said, "Hey, Ira."

He turned around and gave me his slow, quiet look. "Hey, Ellen Grae. I wuz hopin' you'd come by to see me this mornin'. I saw you yistiddy when you come on the train."

"You did? I didn't see you. Why didn't you holler?"

"They wuz people around. Ellen Grae, I got me a goat now."

"Oh, Ira, that's wonderful!"

"When can you come and see her?"

"I don't know. Maybe Sunday after church. I'll get Grover to come with me. I brought back a whole pile of books with me. If you want me to I'll bring one when I come and read you a story. What's your goat's name?"

"Missouri."

"Missouri? That's a funny name for a goat."

"My mother's name wuz Missouri," Ira explained softly, setting two waxed paper bags of boiled peanuts up on the counter. "My goat reminds me of my mother. Did I ever tell you what happened to my mother, Ellen Grae?"

I laid my quarter on the counter and waited for Ira to lay back a nickel change but he didn't. Which wasn't unusual. Ira didn't know how to make change. If you handed him a dollar for one bag of peanuts he'd keep the whole thing. But, by the same token, if you only handed him a penny for a half dozen bags that was all right too. So, if you traded with him for any length of time, things kind of evened themselves out.

"Yes, you told me what happened to your mother, Ira. Listen, I have to go now. Mrs. McGruder and I just came down to the train station to meet Rosemary.

When Grover and I come over Sunday afternoon I'll read to you."

"She died in the swamp, she and her husband. While they wuz tryin' to run away from me. They had 'em this ol' rattler in a box and they wuz draggin' me alongside an' pokin' at him with a stick but instead of bitin' me like he wuz suppose' to, he stuck his ol' head out 'n bit 'em. They swoll up and threshed around some afterward but they wa'n't nothin' I could do for 'em. We wuz too far back in the swamp. So I buried 'em 'longside of that ol' snake. I killed the snake first so he wouldn't bite 'em no more. I didn't tell you 'bout this before, did I, Ellen Grae?"

"No, I reckon this is the first time, Ira. Listen, I'll see you Sunday." I picked up the two bags of peanuts and started to turn away and leave but something in the way Ira looked caused me to turn back. "Listen, Ira, you feel all right, don't you? You aren't sick or anything, are you?"

For a second I thought there were tears on Ira's black lashes but it was only the sun glinting on them. He said, "No, I'm not sick, Ellen Grae. Just tuckered out from talkin' so much."

Poor Ira. He has these hallucinations.

ROSEMARY ARRIVED, her same old gloomy self. As soon as we got back to the McGruders' she started in with her griping. "Well, I can see that nothing much has changed," she commented, flouncing herself around our bedroom with such vigor that the lace of her pink pants showed. "Even that crack on the ceiling's the same. I wish somebody'd tell me why I can't stay home and go to school and be comfortable instead of having to come down here and do it. How much gum have you got in your mouth, Ellen Grae?"

"Four sticks. You want a piece?"

"Oh, God," Rosemary said with a lot of fervor.

I perched myself on the footrail of my bed. "Don't swear, Rosemary. The reason you're here is the same reason I'm here. Our parents are divorced and our fathers have to put us in charge of somebody they can trust. And they trust Mrs. McGruder because she went to the same high school your father and my father did, and she's a nice, homey woman who'll teach us manners and see to it that we get educated and won't corrupt our morals."

"Oh, Ellen Grae, I know all that. Will you please stop smacking that gum? Spit it out. You're making me nervous."

"Everything makes you nervous. Is that a new ring you have on, Rosemary?"

"Yes. My father bought it for me as a going-away present. He's going to send me a watch for my birthday."

"My you're lucky. I wish I had a rich father. But I

reckon to be rich you've got to want to be and Jeff doesn't. I reckon he'll die penniless in a garret."

"A what?"

"A garret. One of those places where people put all their old magazines and other stuff they're tired of. People die in them. *All* artists die in garrets."

"I *wish* Mr. McGruder would fix that crack in the ceiling," Rosemary said irritably. "He *is* still here, isn't he? Have you seen him?"

"I saw him yesterday right after I got here. He was roller-skating out on the sidewalk in front of the house."

Rosemary turned and stared at me. "I'm talking about Mr. McGruder. Are you?"

"Of course. That's who you asked me about, isn't it? He was roller-skating on one skate which that dumb kid next door had left out on the sidewalk. To-day he's in bed. The doctor said he might have to be put in traction."

"In what?"

"Traction. You know. Where they hoist one leg up and attach it to the ceiling? Jeff had to be put in traction once. He couldn't even scratch himself. Grace and I had to do it for him. That's before she and Jeff got a divorce."

"How disgusting. My father wouldn't ask me to scratch him even if he was dying. My father would never dream of letting me see him with one leg fas-

tened to the ceiling. You've got a peculiar family,
Ellen Grae."

"I know it. For centuries all of us Derryberrys have
been peculiar. We can't help ourselves."

"I told my father that you called your parents by
their first names and he couldn't believe it. Please
brush your hair out of your eyes, Ellen Grae. The
way it hangs down like that makes me nervous. Why
do you let it do it?"

"I don't. It just does. You should see Grace's. It's
worse than mine. If Jeff ever sells a painting maybe
I'll ask for the money to have some big fat curls put in.
Like yours. But for right now I guess I'll just have to
slop along like I am. Mrs. McGruder dyed the curtains in here. Did you notice?"

"Hideous. They remind me of measles. At home
we have everything white. Even the rugs and chairs."

"I saw a white chair once. In a doctor's office. I
almost wept it was so beautiful. The doctor said he'd
never seen anybody get so emotional over a piece of
furniture. They had to pry me away from it."

Rosemary's smile was pale. "Oh, honestly, Ellen
Grae."

"It's the truth. It took the nurse and Jeff and the
doctor, all three of them, to pry me away from it. The
doctor said if I was younger he might be able to understand it but as it was, my case had him baffled. He
wanted to call in a psychiatrist but Jeff didn't have

any money. All he had was a picture of a light pole he'd painted and the doctor didn't want that so we had to leave. When we got home Jeff got out a can of paint and took one of our old brown chairs and painted it nice, shiny white and for a while I was comforted. Poor Jeff. I'm afraid he'll never amount to much of anything. He just doesn't have enough education. The Sorbonne didn't teach him how to do anything except paint and speak foreign languages. Does your father ever speak to you in a foreign language, Rosemary?"

"Of course not. He's an American."

"Yes, I know that but I just thought that he might have picked up a few foreign words somewhere. Of course in his business I guess it wouldn't do him any good even if he had. People who borrow money want you to lend it to them in American, don't they? I told Jeff about your father being manager for a finance company but I wish I hadn't. It just made him feel inferior. Listen, Rosemary, aren't you going to unpack? There are plenty of hangers. I only used six. Want me to help you?"

Rosemary's thick, white face filled with impatient contempt. "Thanks but no thanks. Your hands are never clean enough to suit me. At home when Helen —she's our maid—hangs up my clothes I always make her wash her hands first. I wish I could have this room to myself. I'll be thirteen my next birthday and I think it's a positive disgrace that I have to room with a little eleven-year-old kid."

"I think it's a disgrace too, Rosemary. I know it's harder on you than it is on me but I guess we'll just have to make the best of it. Actually, except for the way you twitch and mutter in your sleep and the way you move your lips when you read I really don't mind sharing this room with you, Rosemary."

"I don't move my lips when I read."

"Yes, you do. But maybe I have some bad habits that you don't like too. I tell you what. I'll list all the things you do that I don't like on a piece of paper and you list all the things I do that you don't like on a piece of paper, and we'll exchange papers and each of us will take steps, and maybe we'll get along better than we did last year. Okay?"

Rosemary showed me the whites of her eyes but she said, "Okay. I think we'd better wait until after lunch to do it though because my list isn't going to be just three things like muttering and twitching and moving lips. I've got a long string of things I don't like about you. It'll take me at least thirty minutes to put them all down."

That was an exaggeration but her list, when she finally completed it and with her eyebrows raised to haughty peaks, handed it to me, *was* startling. It complained that my books were everywhere, even under the bed, and that I kept her awake chortling over them or grumbling or making squeaks hopping in and out of bed to run over and consult the dictionary.

It deplored the fact that I didn't share her passion for soap and water, a tidy dresser top, brushed hair with ribbons in it to keep it from flopping, petticoats so that nobody'd ever suspect that I had pants and legs underneath, Sunday school, her father's photograph, clean, polite boys, conversation, dress-up parties, and love movies. It bemoaned the fact that I didn't look like a girl, that I was always eating cheese which made my breath stink, that I used words even when they didn't fit just to impress people and that my choice of friends embarrassed her.

"Which of my friends embarrass you?" I asked.

She gave me a slippery, sidelong look that was supposed to convey something but didn't.

"That crazy Ira, for one."

"Ira's not crazy."

"If he isn't why doesn't he talk to people?"

"He does. He talks to me."

"Ha! I'll bet he's never said one word to you that made any sense. Even his parents couldn't stand him because he's so crazy. They ran away and left him. Everybody in this town knows that."

"Which of my other friends embarrass you, Rosemary?"

"That dumb old Grover."

"Grover's not dumb."

"Sure he is; he should be a grade ahead of you but he isn't. He's twelve and still only in the sixth grade, same as you. Why is that?"

"Because when his mother killed herself he stayed out of school for a year. You shouldn't say mean things about Grover, Rosemary. He says nice things about you."

"What does he say about me?" Rosemary demanded with dark suspicion.

I tried to think fast but the only thing that I could make pop into my mind was a textbook phrase that Jeff had laboriously taught me. *He is glad that you have so much money.* "Il est heureux que vous ayez tant d'argent," I said in French and threw myself backward on the bed, making myself shake with forced laughter.

Rosemary's face puckered and I think she would have started to bawl if Mrs. McGruder hadn't come in just then and said how would we like to take a ride with her out to the chicken ranch and get eggs?

ROSEMARY IS a matutinophobe and I'm a matutinophile. I jump out of bed with a song in my heart every morning. Even if it's raining I'm glad. But this morning it wasn't. The dawn was cool with a colorless sky and a silver mist hanging between the trees. There was the feel of Saturday and the smell of a completed summer in the air. Beyond the McGruders' gate the road stretched out like a ribbon, dry and brown. At the end of the road is the gaunt house where Grover lives.

He never acts surprised to see me. With two cold biscuit and ham sandwiches in his hand he came to the screen door and blinked his brown eyes a couple of times and then came out on the porch and handed me one of the sandwiches and said, "Hey, Ellen Grae. You back?"

"No, this is my ghost come to visit you."

He searched the inside of one ear with a brown finger. "Why you pantin'?"

"I'm not panting. I'm just breathing. Walking down here I breathed three hundred and fourteen times. I controlled it though so it didn't hurt me. I know a girl who didn't control her breathing and breathed so hard the wrong way that her eyeballs fell out."

"I didn't know there was a wrong way and a right way to breathe."

"Sure there is. Singers and people who make speeches all the time go to school to learn to breathe right."

Grover placed one hand on his bare stomach and breathed. "I think I'd rather be deaf than blind."

"Who's blind?"

"The girl whose eyeballs fell out. Didn't you say her eyeballs fell out?"

"Yes, but she's not blind."

"She isn't?"

"No. She would have been but fortunately her father's a famous eye surgeon and he quick got two eyeballs from somebody else in the hospital where he works who'd just died and put them in this girl's sockets and she can see just as good as ever. The only thing is in his frantic haste he overlooked the fact that one of the eyeballs was green and the other black. She's in the movies now and her father isn't a doctor any more. They live in Hollywood, California now. Listen, Grover, this ham is so salty I'm about to gag. Could I have a drink of water?"

"It's well water," Grover warned. "Last year you said *that* made you gag."

"I know I did but that was last year. I've changed my mind about a lot of things since then. One of them's water. Did you know that country people live longer than city people just because they drink pure water?"

"No, I didn't know that."

"Well, they do. You ever see a country person with calcified bones?"

"No, I don't think so."

"Of course not. But all city people have them—

even me. What causes them is all the stuff they put in the water tanks to purify it. A man fell in our city water tank last Christmas Eve day while he was up there painting a sign that said Joy To The World on the side of it, and they didn't find his body until it had all come apart and now practically everybody in the city is calcified."

In three bites Grover consumed his sandwich, left the porch, and walked across the yard to the spring-fed well and pumped and came back with a tin dipper of water and handed it to me. While I drank he scratched himself.

"I fixed the boat so it doesn't leak any more and I got me a flag and some oars for it now. You want to go fishing?"

"I reckon I do. I left a note for Mrs. McGruder. She'll jaw at me when I get back but by that time it'll be too late. Let's go."

"Wait," Grover said and went back into the house and was gone a couple of minutes. When he came back out he had his shirt and shoes on, and carried a whole roasted chicken and two bananas in a plastic bag. "It's all I could find," he apologized. "But it'll taste good about noon. Let's go."

The parched fields between Grover's house and the river lay passive, brittle underfoot, and filled with the dusty scent of dried roots and dehydrated underbrush. The sun climbed steadily, clean and hot. A

cloud of black gnats found us and Grover grabbed my
hand and we ran, panting and sweating and stirring up
little puffs of choking dirt with our feet, until we
reached the river bank. Sweet, cool air rushed up and
out to meet us. The boat, tied to a water oak, bobbed
with the motion of the water. Grover had painted the
outside of it gray and the inside a glistening red. The
flag, attached to the stern, made it look official. Two
cane poles, a bait bucket, and a small shovel rested
beneath a piece of canvas in its bottom.

Grover took off his shoes and slid down and climbed
into the boat and stored the chicken and bananas and
returned with the bucket and shovel. We dug pink
worms from his worm bed and deposited them in the
bucket along with plenty of damp, black earth. I lost
a few of them getting in the boat—the bucket clanged
against the side—and Grover gave me a look and muttered something about girls being clumsy but we
didn't have words like we sometimes did when he said
that because I swallowed my temper.

The river, broad and tranquil and gently curving,
welcomed us like an old friend. We paddled out into
the middle of it and Grover, trying to look and act
nautical, stood up in the bow, shaded his eyes with
his hand even though there wasn't much sun because
of the overhanging trees, scanned the water and both
banks, and said, "Rest your oar, Ellen Grae."

I rested my oar.

"I'm going to catch a fish," Grover said. "Hand me a worm."

I handed him a worm.

"Aren't you going to fish?" he inquired, wrestling around with one of the cane poles and a hook and the worm.

"Not for the nonce. For the nonce I just want to sit here and let nature exert her wonderful powers of healing o'er my bruised spirit."

Grover lowered his pole into the water and sat down, placing his back against one side of the boat's hull and planting his feet against the other, preparing for a heavy strike. "What's it bruised from?"

"My spirit? My spirit's not bruised, Grover. How could it be? I was just trying that out on you to see what you'd say. What'd it make you think of when I said it?"

"A lady who's dying," Grover said unexpectedly. "What's it make you think of?"

"A monk with a hood over his face weeping for humanity."

"Do monks weep for humanity?"

"Some of them do. I knew a monk once who spent his whole life doing nothing but weeping for humanity. All he did was sit around in doorways and beg alms to keep his poor wracked body together and weep for humanity. The sounds that came out of him were terrible. I'll never forget them. The day before

he died he gave me his Bible. I'll show it to you sometime. He was from Scotland and in the Book of Psalms
he left a piece of pressed heather. I guess the poor
thing yearned for his country, even to the last. I had to
sneak the Bible out of the sanitarium; he was tuber-
cular."

Grover wrapped a denim leg around the pole and
with a dirt-crusted toe jiggled it. He turned a solemn,
brown gaze on me. "I've never seen a monk but I
knew a lady who came from Scotland once. She was
born with her head in her arm pit. She told me that
lots of people over there are born that way. It's some
kind of a curse or something. She was sure ugly. Nobody but me could stand to look at her. Not even her
husband. He used to pay me fifty cents a week to take
food to her. She died from eating too much peanut
butter; when they embalmed her they had to stop when
they got to her stomach because it was glued together
with peanut butter. At her funeral her husband
fainted and fell in the grave with her and all of her
relatives who'd come over from Scotland to pay their
last respects fell to their knees in the mud. They all
looked like this lady I'm telling you about and had to
spend the night at the funeral home because the hotel
wouldn't rent them a room. The funeral director said
they cried all night long but said it wasn't like any
crying he'd ever heard before. They were polite
though and didn't make any mess and paid him and

every once in a while now he gets a box from them with sweaters in them. The only thing is the neck holes are always in the wrong place. I guess they keep forgetting that everybody's not born with their head in their arm pit."

I studied the cypress trees on the river banks. Festooned with Spanish moss they looked like old, gray-bearded men. Two birds sailing wing-to-wing overhead dipped low and one of them made droppings on the bow of the boat. With a look of bland contentment Grover sucked his cheeks.

"That's the most utter story I ever heard," I said after some thought.

"Whad'ya mean, utter?"

"I mean utter. Put anything after it you want but it's utter."

"Then there was this other man I knew from Scotland who ate oat cakes all the time. Nothing but oat cakes. And roamed the moors at night, mourning."

"For his departed ancestors, I suppose."

"Yes. For his departed ancestors. One night he asked me to go along. It was raining sheets and black as soot and every once in awhile there'd be this great big bolt of lightning——"

"——that tore up trees and hurled bodies through the air but you and your friend stepped out in your long black capes——"

"——and roamed the moor all night. Afterward I

had pneumonia and had to stay in bed for three days and in my delirium I told my father where I'd been to get sick and at first he didn't believe me. He said there wasn't anybody-around here like that . . . that I'd dreamed it all——"

"——but one night there was a tapping at the window and your father went to see what it was and there stood your friend from Scotland in his black cape."

"Yes," Grover said, grinning.

"Grover, those are the two worst stories I ever heard in my whole life. You certainly don't expect me to believe them, do you?"

"Why not? They're as true as most of the ones you tell me."

"I beg your pardon?"

"I wish a two-pound catfish would come along and grab hold of this hook," he said. "I just wrote a poem. You want to hear it?"

"A poem? I didn't know you could write poetry."

"I didn't either until just a minute ago. But here's what I wrote:

IN A DOORWAY SAT A HUNK OF A MONK.

HE WAS PRAYING AND BEGGING AND STUNK.

HE STANK BECAUSE HE DRUNK.

HE DRUNK BECAUSE OF ELLEN GRAE'S BUNK!

Without appetite the river's smooth tongue pushed and licked at the stern and sides of the boat. Off our bow a fish jumped but Grover ignored it. "Did you like my poem?" he asked with a clear, innocent expression and both of us burst out laughing.

It was good out there on the river with the sunlight dappling the brown water and the soft, intermingling odors of the forest all around. We saw two otters sunning themselves on the river bank and a blue heron standing stiff-legged on a cypress knee. Grover stood up and hooted at it but it didn't move. Far off to our right a giant bullfrog thumped out a throaty basso lament and was answered by a timid, soprano peep. We reached the bend in the river and I sat up straight and looked hard toward Ira's shack and saw Missouri tugging on a towel or something that was hanging from the clothesline, but Ira wasn't anywhere about.

"I been readin' about buried treasure," Grover said, plying his oar with red-faced energy. "I'll bet there's lots of it around here just waitin' for somebody to come along and dig it up. Let's you and me bring a coupla shovels out here next Saturday and root around. Want to?"

"Sure. We'll bring Ira along. He can be our guide. He knows this swamp better than anybody. You got him to talk to you yet?"

"Some. I took him and his goat fishin' about a month ago. He talked to me some then."

"What'd he talk about?"

"Nothin'. His goat's name is Missouri. He said he named it after his mother."

On Sunday Grover and I didn't get to go to Ira's place so that I could read to him because it rained. We didn't go to Sunday school or church either because Mrs. McGruder was coming down with a cold and Mr. McGruder was still limping from his roller-skating accident.

For dinner we had roast leg of lamb with mint jelly. Rosemary griped.

In the afternoon everybody except me took a nap. I read a book and watched Rosemary, who sleeps with her eyes partly open which can be a little frightening in the dead of night but which in the daytime is interesting. The lower ovals of them, with stiff fans of brown hair above and beneath them, gleam whitely and with every breath roll and turn in their watery sockets. Her mouth, painted a cold, gleaming purple with lipstick, which she isn't allowed to wear in Mrs. McGruder's presence, pulls back from her teeth in secret mirth.

About two o'clock I finished my book and the rain stopped and I went up to the attic and opened a window and leaned out and watched a rainbow appear. The glow from it touched the meadows, lacquering them with gold and the foot of it dipped deep into the swamp beyond.

CAME LABOR DAY which Mrs. McGruder believes in. She and Mr. McGruder washed every window and hosed down the outside of the house.

Rosemary and I polished all of our shoes and examined all of our dresses and slips and pants for missing buttons and open seams and tears. We straightened our room and washed our hair. To make it shine I put vinegar on mine and Rosemary put a cream rinse on hers.

"Grover and I are going treasure hunting next Saturday," I told her. "You wouldn't want to come along, would you?"

"No thank you."

"You'd have a good time. It's lots of fun rowing up and down the river."

She anchored a fat curl to one temple with four hairpins. A thin spark of interest came into her face. "Well, I *might* be interested when the time comes. I wouldn't have to help row, would I?"

"No. Ira's going to come with us. He and Grover will do the rowing."

The interest died. She said, "Oh. Oh, I don't think I want to go, Ellen Grae. You wouldn't want to come home when I'd want to and the sun's bad for my skin. But thank you for asking me. Thank you a lot."

Came Tuesday and we went off to school. I took

my petticoat off when I got there and stuck it in my desk. Mrs. McGruder believes in lots of starch and I don't; I like my clothes limply comfortable.

Right away we got down to the business of getting educated. For our first homework assignment Miss Daniels, the new English teacher, said for us to write a short story and use the words allege and accusation and akimbo in it. So that night I wrote a story about Albert, a seamy man from the Allegheny Mountains who was alleged to be mean and brutal but who was really, in truth, very lovely and gentle. One day when he realized the true meaning of all the accusations the town people had been making against him he climbed up to the top of a blue hill and stood there, his arms akimbo, and swore his revenge.

Miss Daniels said that my story met all of the requirements and she kept me after school so that we could talk about it.

"Of what was Albert being accused?" she inquired. "That point wasn't quite clear to me."

"It wasn't quite clear to me either," I confessed. "I just knew there had to be some accusations for something so I stuck it in there."

"What makes you think a hill is blue?" she asked. "Have you ever seen a blue hill?"

"Yes, ma'am. I've seen hills all colors. Green, black, brown, purple. But I believe the blue ones are the prettiest."

She said, "Your handwriting is really quite terrible. I think we must work on that."

"Yes, ma'am."

"You must learn to keep your margins neat and write straight across and form each letter. Letters are not supposed to lean on one another. Each is supposed to stand on its own."

"Yes, ma'am."

She touched the white froth that was her collar. "But I liked your blue hill," she said.

Before Grace and Jeff got their divorce we always went to a Chinese restaurant on Thursday nights and then went home to do the wash and hang it on pulley lines. If there was a night breeze it would flap and keep us awake. We were up so high with just building tops all around and the washes of other moneyless people hanging like tired skeletons on other swinging lines. But Thursday night at the McGruders' usually brought Pigs in the Blanket, which was hamburger baked in biscuit dough, or Pigs in the Sheet, which was hamburger boiled in cabbage leaves, and then afterward Rosemary and I studied. We were not allowed to watch television.

Friday was general assembly day at school. Sometimes, after all the announcements and stuff, somebody with talent would get up on the stage and perform. There was this boy who had a sousaphone and knew how to play it but somebody poured water in it and when he came strutting out and started to play for us no music came out—just gurgles. Everybody laughed.

SATURDAY, STILL AND YELLOW and hot, arrived. The minute I went to the window and looked out at it I knew that it was going to be different. A hummingbird with a ruby throat and an emerald head hovered motionless above a pale hibiscus blossom, his wing tips whistling. As I watched he delicately settled himself on the flower, stuck his bill into it and drank. Beneath the hibiscus bush the grass with droplets of night moisture on it sparkled green.

Rosemary's eyes were completely closed and her mouth, without lipstick, looked clean and kind.

In the kitchen Mr. McGruder, who was the only one up besides me, set two buckwheat pancakes in front of me and without thinking I ate them both. He wanted to know why I was up so early.

"It's not early," I said. "It's six o'clock. Grover and I are going treasure hunting."

Mr. McGruder looked vague and hid himself behind the morning paper.

"Ira is going with us," I said. "We'll be gone most all day. Will you tell Mrs. McGruder so she won't worry?"

Deep in his paper Mr. McGruder said, "Sure."

"Is it okay if I fix some sandwiches and stuff for our lunch?"

"Sure. Go ahead."

"And can I borrow your square shovel?"

"Help yourself."

Mr. McGruder is a very generous man.

Between the McGruders' house and Grover's there lay a shimmering calm. The sky, streaked with pennants of bright rose, was motionless. A cardinal swung from a streamer of Spanish moss. There was the smell of mimosa and dog fennel and flowering honeysuckle in the air.

Outside of Grover's house I hollered for him and he came trotting. "Hey, Ellen Grae. You bring everything I told you to? You didn't forget to bring Mr. McGruder's shovel, did you?"

"Oh, Grover, I sure did. This thing you see here in my hand is a wand."

Until we paddled down the river and collected Ira and Missouri there wasn't anybody for Grover to take charge of except me, but he pulled his shoulders back and squared his face and clipped out commands. I was ordered to carry the shovel, my sack of lunch, a coil of rope, a bottle of insect repellent, a small first-aid kit, and a jar of foul-smelling salve which had healing powers. Grover carried another sack of lunch, another shovel, and a hatchet to hack our way through the forest. I was ordered not to talk—to save my energy for the walk to the river and the boat. So in silence we set out.

The shovel was heavy and I had to keep shifting it from one hand to the other. The muscles in my upper arms quivered from the strain. A covey of fat-chested quail flashed across our path. Strong and gathering heat, the sun climbed. A bug stung me on my cheek and when we got to the boat Grover put ammonia on it. "If you'd watch where you're going you wouldn't get stung," he said. "Does it hurt?"

"Oh no. It feels good. I like being stung by bugs."

He put the cap back on the ammonia bottle. "Don't talk. Save your energy for rowing."

We rowed down the river and when we got to the bend altered our course and put in and picked up Ira and Missouri. Missouri came into the boat without being coaxed and when Ira climbed in and sat down in the bow, went to him and laid her head in his lap. Ira took a lump of sugar from his shirt pocket and offered it to her and she looked at him and flicked her red tongue out and gathered it into her mouth and swallowed it whole.

"I washed her yistiddy," Ira said, his black eyes full of light. "Say somethin' to her, Ellen Grae."

I said, "Hey, Missouri." And she left Ira and came to me, pushing her wiry body against my knees.

"Let's shove off," Grover said, his mouth square and

hard. And Ira, without being told, moved to the stern and took up an oar and dipped it into the water and with beautiful ease we moved out of the cove and back into the river. Like a dog, Missouri lifted her head and pointed her nose into the wind. I put my hand on her clean, white back and she grunted trustingly. Her horns, curving gently backward, gleamed like polished glass.

Grover, in the bow of the boat, said, "How far down river you reckon we ought to go, Ira?"

"A piece," Ira answered.

So, gliding through the brown water, we went on down river a piece to where it narrowed and the sunlight struggled to get through the dark, overhanging trees and the swamp rose up on both sides of us, dank and cool and spiked with clumps of coarse grass and wild fern and stumps. The land looked solid but Ira, with a look of unease, said, "Ellen Grae?"

"What, Ira?"

"We best go back a piece."

"Why? What's wrong with it here?"

Ira turned his head and looked at Missouri. "We best go back a piece."

Grover laid his oar aside, hung his head over the side of the boat and splashed water into his face. "We'll go back pretty soon, Ira. As soon as we eat and have a look around. Break out the lunch, Ellen Grae."

I broke out the lunch and divided it four ways. Missouri refused a drumstick but crunched happily on an apple.

"Where you reckon all this treasure we're supposed to look for is?" I asked Grover. "If you ask me I don't think any of it's back here. This is just swamp."

"Sure it's swamp. That's what we want. Swamp. In the olden days, before the government made them go live on reservations, Indians used to live back here. I got a book from the library and read up on it and found out."

"Found out what?"

"That they didn't have any money then. They used fishhooks made out of gold for money."

"And you figure they left some of these hooks behind?"

Grover's brown eyes spurned my realism. "I figure they might have. But we aren't out here just to look for gold fishhooks. We'll take anything we can find. The Spaniards used to own this land before America did and they were rich. But they were always fightin' with the Americans and the Indians. If some of them had to run off in a hurry you think they'd stop to drag all their stuff along?"

"Gee, Grover, I don't know. I never thought about it."

Grover put a finger between two shirt buttons and reached inside and scratched. A strange kind of soft, sweet excitement crept into his eyes. "We aren't too

far from the ocean. A lot of Spanish ships used to be
wrecked off of this coast and the sailors used to come
in here and hide while they were waitin' for other ships
to come by and pick them up. They buried stuff
from their ships when they couldn't take it along.
Silverware and money and jewelry. We'd be rich if
we could find just one piece, Ellen Grae."

"How do we know where to dig?"

"You look for mounds and sunken places. Some
treasure hunters use mine detectors but they cost
about twenty dollars even in army surplus stores."

Ira said, "We best go back a piece, Ellen Grae."

"We'll go pretty soon, Ira. But first we want to
look around a little. You know this part of the swamp,
don't you? You've been here before, haven't you?"

Ira's half smile was shy and slow and uncertain. "I
bin here before I think."

"Sure you have," Grover said, hearty and vigorous
and eager. "So you take Missouri and go first and Ellen
Grae and me'll follow. Look for us a good place to
dig. Watch out for mounds and sunken places, Ira."

Missouri, anticipating, went to stand in the bow of
the boat and Ira went up and climbed off, and then
lifted her to the bank. They stood there for a second
and then Missouri lifted her head and sniffed and
made a noise and Ira, with his hand, gave her his con-
sent to go. She made another noise and broke away
from him and wheeled and streaked off through the

dense swamp growth, her dainty legs flashing. Ira followed her. In just a minute or two they were lost from our sight.

The forest sighed and rustled and murmured.

Grover said, "He didn't want to stay here for some reason. But I think our chances are as good here as they are anywhere else; maybe better. At least it's not as marshy here as it is on back a ways. Ira'll find us a good likely lookin' spot. He knows what we're after. He's not as dumb as some people think he is. Break out your shovel, Ellen Grae."

I broke out my shovel.

"You're not like most girls," Grover said. "I don't have to tell you that if you're going to look for buried treasure you got to get out of the boat."

I laid the shovel across my shoulder and by myself struggled out of the bobbing boat. Grover, with the other shovel and the hatchet, followed.

"Watch where you're goin'," Grover ordered. "Which way did Ira go?"

"This way. Lordy, it's hot."

"It's gonna get hotter. We oughta get somethin' done before the heat tuckers us out."

All around us the swamp lay deep in its ancient silence. Making our own path as we went, we came upon a stand of grass containing a ground nest full of eggs so glossy they looked like porcelain and very deep in color. Grover knelt and examined them. "Probably ducks," he said. "Ira might know. Where the heck is he?"

I peered through the trees ahead but didn't see Ira. I hollered for him but just the echo of my own voice, high and eerie, answered.

"These eggs are the prettiest I've ever seen," Grover said, engrossed in them. "They look like they've been dyed. I'd sure like to know what kind they are. Go on up ahead a little, Ellen Grae. Ira's up there doin' somethin'. Tell him I want him to come back here and look at these eggs."

I laid my shovel down and tightened the belt to my pants. "There might be quicksand around here."

"Ain't no quicksand around here. Go on."

Ten minutes later I found Ira standing beside a sunken place in the earth's floor. Missouri, her tail a stiff white plume, stood motionless beside him. The sun had penetrated the treetops and lay in a bright pool on the sunken place, the man, and the goat.

Ira had his back to me and didn't turn until I went up to him and laid my hand on his arm.

I said, "Hey, Ira, what's the matter? Why are you just standing here? Grover's found a nest full of eggs and wants you to come back and look at them. Come on."

He looked down at me and I saw then the pain and

sorrow in him. There were tears in his eyes. He said, "Ellen Grae, you remember I told you what happened to my mother and her husband?"

"Yes, Ira, I remember but——"

"They had 'em this snake in a box and they wuz draggin' me alongside and pokin' at him with a stick . . ."

"Ira, I remember! I told you I remember! I don't want to hear about it anymore now! Come on, let's go back to where Grover is."

". . . but instead of bitin' me like he wuz suppose' to he stuck his head out and bit them."

I looked at the sunken place and my stomach shifted.

Missouri made a sound in her throat.

"I didn't know what to do, Ellen Grae. We didn't come here in any boat. I didn't know what to do so I . . ."

"Ira, I told you I didn't want to hear about it anymore! You've told me about it a thousand times and I'm sick of it! Come on! Grover's waiting for us. He wants you to look at some duck eggs."

". . . I buried 'em," he whispered and stepped back away from me and out of the pool of sunlight.

My voice didn't belong to me. It had a bottomless calm. It said, "All right, Ira, let's go back now. Grover's found a nest full of eggs and wants you to look at them."

He let me take him by the hand then and we walked away from the place. Missouri trotted beside us. She didn't look back and neither did Ira nor I.

Ira couldn't identify the eggs. He said he had seen lots of them in the swamp but didn't know what kind they were.

I said that I had a headache, one of the worst I'd ever had in my whole life, and wanted to go home.

Grover wasn't very sympathetic. He said it looked to him like I could have got my headache over with the day before if I had to have one. He wanted to know why we had to be in such an all-fired hurry. He got very mad at me.

IN THE SWAMP, beneath a blanket of dirt, with nothing between them and it, lay Ira's mother and her husband put there by Ira, and I alone knew this dark and heavy secret. How was I going to manage to keep this to myself? Little secrets weren't hard to keep but this one wasn't little. It was threatening. If I didn't keep it what would happen to my friend Ira who had never on purpose harmed a soul in his whole life? Would he be sent to the crazy house or to jail?

Were their faces raised in their death sleep to the rain and the sun? How far beneath the earth's surface were they buried? Far enough so that the wind wouldn't blow away their blanket and expose them? Oh, surely Ira would have had enough sense to bury them deep—he had a lot of primitive intelligence.

But it wasn't right. Dead people, even bad ones, belonged in cemeteries with markers at their heads to let people know when they had been born and when they had died. Maybe there was somebody besides Ira who had cared about them and, if they knew, would want to come and stand beside their cradle and cry and put flowers. But no one would ever know about these two except Ira and me. They would lie there in the swamp, still and cold, forever with the snake coiled beside them, the last of his evils done.

I did my best not to think about it. I crammed my mind with all kinds of things—stuff I didn't even care about, hoping that if I filled it full enough and kept it busy enough it would forget. But slyly the secret clung.

It brought a change in me. Came a hunger for food which had only been of small interest before.

"You act like you've got a tapeworm," Rosemary said. "The way you stuff yourself. All that food you eat you ought to weigh a ton but, my, you're skinny. I wouldn't be as skinny as you for anything."

And came this thirst for sleep. "You used to get up with the roosters," Mrs. McGruder commented. "Now I can't force you out of bed. Are you sure you're not sick?"

"No, ma'am, I'm not sick. I'm just tired."

Mr. McGruder, who was a male nurse in his youth, said that my lethargy could be diabetes or some other serious disease.

I was hustled off to the doctor. His hair grew in red powder puffs on each side of his head but none on top and his palms, soft and dry, whispered when he rubbed them together. The toes of his shoes were a dark, brilliant ebony.

We sat down in his white office and he said, "All right now, Ellen Grae."

"Sir?"

"Do you hurt anywhere?"

"No, sir."

"Not one little pain or ache anywhere?"

"No, sir."

"Mrs. McGruder tells me that all you want to do lately is sleep. Is that true?"

"I reckon it is."

"Why is this do you suppose?"

"I don't know. Maybe it's because I don't have anything to stay awake for."

This doctor had very white, very beautiful teeth. When he smiled I could see that two of his back ones were hooked on to two of his side ones with tiny, silver prongs. He said, "Do you go to the bathroom a lot?"

"Sometimes. If I drink a lot of water I do."

"And do you drink a lot of water?"

"Sometimes."

"Are you thirsty now?"

"No, sir."

"Are you sleepy now?"

"No, sir."

The doctor showed me his silver prongs again. He said, "Well, I think we'd better have a look at you."

Naturally he didn't find anything because there wasn't anything. My tonsils were the right size, I didn't have rales in my chest, my kneecaps and elbows jumped when hit with his little hammer signifying that I had the proper reflexes. I had the right number of red corpuscles and white corpuscles in my blood and I didn't have any sugar in my urine. He couldn't look inside my skull and see the trouble that was hidden deep there, visible to no man, a tricky, brooding piece of knowledge, swarthy and insidious. He wrote out two prescriptions and I went with Mrs. Mc-Gruder to the drugstore and waited in a booth with her while the druggist filled them.

She ordered two cherry smashes and while we were drinking them she said, "Well, I'm glad there's nothing physically wrong with you."

"Yes, ma'am, I'm glad there's nothing physically wrong with me too."

"But I think if I had my choice I'd rather be physically disturbed than mentally. What about you?"

"I think that'd be better. Yes, ma'am."

"Your manners are improving," she said. "I'm glad to see that."

"Thank you, ma'am."

"But I don't know. I kind of liked you the other way too. I haven't had a good story out of you lately," she said.

"No, ma'am. I don't know any."

"You remember the one you told me about Fortis Alonzo Gridley?"

"Yes, ma'am, I remember."

Her green eyes had corners of shadow in them. "I told it to the girls at my bridge club and all of them thought it was very funny."

"It wasn't a true story, Mrs. McGruder. All of it was a lie. I made it up."

The shadows in her eyes came out of the corners and darkened all of the white and green in them and her voice softened the way it did when anybody in her house was sick and needed attention. She said, "No, it wasn't a lie. It was a story. You tell wonderful stories, Ellen Grae."

"I don't think I do but thank you."

Mrs. McGruder turned her head and her eyes traveled across the black and white checkerboard floor to

a counter where a girl in a blue smock with a num-
bered button on its front was prettily arranging a
pyramid of pink boxes. She said, "Honey, I wish you'd
tell me what it is that's troubling you."

"Nothing's troubling me, Mrs. McGruder. The
cherry smash was good. I thank you for it."

"Rosemary said she heard you crying in your sleep
last night."

"Well, I don't know why she said that. You know I
never cry even when I'm awake. Tears are useless; I
found that out a long time ago. Jeff taught me. None
of us Derryberrys cry about things."

Mrs. McGruder sighed but she didn't say anything
more. The druggist came with the prescriptions which
were just vitamins and we went home and Mrs.
McGruder baked macaroni and cheese and apple
dumplings for supper and I ate so much that I couldn't
concentrate on my homework afterward and later on,
just before I went to bed, it all came up.

I had this dream about Ira. In it he was sitting on
a stool in a room far away from the river and Missouri and there was sun which lay in bars across his
shoulders and face. His beautiful hair had turned
solid white and looked coarse and his feet, without
any socks on them, had been stuffed into hard, pointed
shoes. In this dream I saw myself go up some steps
which were gray and cold and at the top was a door

with a window in it. I went over to it and rapped on the glass and Ira rose and shuffled over and slid the pane back and peered out at me.

I said, "Hey, Ira. It's me. Ellen Grae."

His black eyes, very dry and very old, regarded me. "You went and told on me," he said. "I didn't think you'd do that, Ellen Grae."

"Oh, Ira, I didn't want to! I'm your friend! Really I am!"

"I thought you wuz," he said. "I thought you wuz my friend but you went and told on me."

"Ira, I had to! You have *got* to understand that! I didn't know they'd put you in here, honest I didn't! You're my friend! I wouldn't ever do anything to hurt you on purpose!"

With a terrible sadness and longing in his face he said, "You wuz my friend. The onliest one I ever had. And you went and told on me. Good-bye, Ellen Grae. Good-bye. Good-bye. Good-bye."

The last thing I remember seeing in the dream was his feet as he turned and limped back to his stool. Above the stiff leather that bound them I saw the ankles puffed, with the bones straining, and I felt the pain in them and in the darkness surrounding my bed there came this sound, clenched and low, which woke me and I realized that I was the one making it. I didn't go back to sleep for fear of other sounds I might make and other dreams I might dream.

At school I saw Grover every day. He said that he had had a chance to do some more reading about buried treasure and where in the United States it might be found and that his first calculations had been wrong. That it wasn't in any swamp or near any swamp.

His interest in it had cooled, he told me one afternoon while we were walking home. "I've got a job now," he said. "I'm learning how to be a veterinarian. My uncle is teaching me and he pays me three dollars every time I work all day. A dollar and a half if I only work till noon. Ellen Grae, are you listening to me?"

"Yes, Grover, I'm listening."

"That's where I was last Saturday. That's why I didn't come and ask you to go fishing or do something else. I had to go out to the country and help my uncle doctor this sick old cow. It took us all day. I didn't even have time to go to the movies. Did you go?"

"No."

"Why didn't you?"

"Because I hate to go to town."

"You never used to. You used to like to go to town. Even if we only had enough money for one bag of peanuts between us you used to like to." The strap around his books didn't look too strong but he took it by the end and swung it around and around. "Friday," he said, his grin buoyant. "I thought it'd never get here. Hey, Ellen Grae, I got me a new rod and reel. My uncle bought it for me. You want to meet me down at the river after a while and try it out?"

"I don't think so, Grover."

"Why not? School's out till Monday. You don't have to do homework tonight. Come on."

"I don't want to go down to the boat, Grover, and if you're going to walk the rest of the way home with me please shut up. You're making my head ache."

Grover stopped swinging the books and for five minutes he stopped talking. A car full of high school kids, giddy with Friday freedom, appeared in the dusty road, speeded past us and somebody threw out an empty Coke bottle. The sun, a scorching ball of white fire, breathing heat and sucking up the earth's moisture, touched the worn-out grass on both sides of the road. Heat waves danced on brown lace fences.

Grover squinted his eyes and looked up into the sun's glare and whistled a tune. He said, "They say a person's crazy if he can look right into the sun without scrooching up his eyes."

"Who says that, Grover?"

"Doctors. I read doctor books all the time. My uncle's got a whole room full of 'em."

"Has he?"

"He studied to be a doctor for humans before he decided that animals were more interesting. He says that animals are cleaner and that when people call other people animals it's a compliment. You should have seen him operate on that old sick cow last Saturday. Her sides were all bloated out about four feet and her eyes were all rolled back in her head and she was staggerin' around like she was drunk when we found her. We had a heck of a time getting her into the back seat of the car so's we could operate on her."

"You put a cow into the back seat of your uncle's car?"

"Well, no, come to think of it we didn't. We couldn't get her in. We had to do it right there on the ground. My uncle gave her a shot to knock her out and I grabbed my instruments and ran up to this farmhouse and boiled them, then I ran back and we put on our rubber gloves and operated. Ellen Grae, you should have seen . . ."

We had reached the McGruders' gate. "Grover," I said. "You'll have to tell me the rest of the story some other time. I'm home now."

"Wait a minute, Ellen Grae."

"So long, Grover. I'll see you."

"I got another real good story to tell you. I'll tell it real fast. We could go up on the porch and sit in the shade while I do it. It'll cheer you up. I don't know what's wrong with you but you look like you need cheering up."

"So long, Grover. I'll see you."

"All right," said Grover, scowling. He turned and

humped off down the road and I turned and opened the gate and went up the walk and the steps and opened the screen door and stepped into the coolness of the house and there, sitting on Mrs. McGruder's chintz sofa, were Grace and Jeff.

THEY STAYED AT the Gingham Inn the name of which, Grace said, was supposed to make people coming in at the train station two blocks away, think of comfortable rooms with braided rugs on the floors and red geraniums in window boxes and homey cleanliness.

"But it's the misnomer of all times," she declared, pulling back the sheets on her bed to better examine the mattress for bedbugs. "Did you remember to ask Mrs. McGruder for a clean fruit jar, Ellen Grae?"

"Yes, ma'am. She gave me two. What are they for?"

"To keep my nylons in. Roaches love nylon and this place is alive with the nasty things. I found that out last year. Since when," she asked, "has ma'am and sir become a part of your vocabulary?"

"I don't know. Since I came back here this time, I guess. I thought it sounded nicer than just answering yes and no."

Grace's eyes, keen and gray and sober, studied me. "You're a nice kid, Ellen Grae. It's too bad you couldn't have inherited some nice, normal parents."

"I think you and Jeff are nice, normal parents, Grace. I like you."

Grace said, "Thank you, dear. We don't deserve it but thank you."

"See any bedbugs?"

"I don't think so. Of course you never can tell until it gets dark. That's when they make their grand entrance." Her hands, without rings and lightly tanned, smoothed the sheets back into place, drew the counterpane. Turning, she said, "Well now, I think we can talk but I think your father should be present while we're doing it. You want to run down the hall and get him, honey? He's in room eighteen."

"What are we going to talk about?" I asked. "What's wrong?"

"We don't know, yet," she answered. "That's why we're here. To find out."

They had come to find out why I ate so much and yet grew skinnier all the time, and why I slept so much and yet was tired all the time, and why I cried in my sleep, and why my grades at school had turned from being A's into C's and why I refused to accompany Rosemary to the movies on Saturday afternoons.

They sat on chairs and I sat on the bed. There was the smell of Grace's clean cologne in the room and Jeff's after-shave lotion and stale furniture wax and molding carpet. There was the sound of water running through pipes and a loud, overhead radio voice. There was this feeling of airless closeness, like just before a storm.

While I was down the hall getting Jeff, Grace had changed her dark dress to a light one and put on fresh lipstick. Her brown hair, drawn back from her face and held with a velvet ribbon, was sweet. She and Jeff gave each other grave smiles. To me Grace said, "Now then, Ellen Grae."

"Ma'am?"

She crossed her beautiful legs. "It's really no use, you know, to put on that bland face with us. We've come to find out what's wrong and we're going to find out what's wrong if we have to sit here all night."

"And I don't want to sit here all night," Jeff said. "After we get our powwow out of the way I want the three of us to go out and find the best restaurant in town, and I want us to eat the best dinner they have to offer, and then I want to take you to the movies. We'll get a loge."

"There isn't anything wrong," I said. "You don't want me to invent something just to satisfy you, do you?"

Jeff examined the palms of his hands. "No, the truth will do. If you don't mind let's have it."

The water in the pipes hammered and the radio voice from the room above quickened to a rich, pleading insistence. At the window a lukewarm breeze stirred the weary curtains. The dream I had had of Ira wept against the walls of my mind.

I said, "There isn't anything wrong. Let's go eat. I'm going to have steak if you can afford it."

"Is it our being divorced?" they asked. "Are you having trouble with that at school?"

"No, I'm not having trouble with your being divorced at school. Is there any ice? Could I have a drink of water, please?"

Grace fixed me a drink of ice and water in a plastic cup. "Your father and I are still very good friends," she said. "And we always will be. You know that, don't you?"

"Yes, I know that."

"Are you worried about one of us re-marrying?"

"No. I think about it sometimes—I know that it might happen sometime but I'm not worried about it. I'm not worried about anything."

"Are you having trouble with Rosemary?" they asked.

"No, I'm not having any trouble with Rosemary. I like her better this year than I did last year even though she's still stuck-up but that isn't her fault. Her father makes her that way."

A smile dawdled at the corners of Jeff's mouth. "We understand you went hunting for lost treasure about three weeks ago."

"Yeah."

"Find anything?"

"Naaah."

"How's Grover?"

"Fine."

"You still like him, don't you?"

"Sure. Of course he's a terrible liar but that doesn't hurt anything. Grover's fine. I like him."

Grace took the ribbon out of her hair. Now there was the beginning of dusk in the room, softly creeping.

Grace pushed her hair back and again fastened the velvet ribbon. The bones in her face stood out suddenly, white and sharp. She said, "How's Ira?"

"Who?"

"Ira. The man who sells peanuts."

"Oh. You mean Ira."

"That's right. How is he?"

"I dunno. I reckon he's all right. He was the last time I saw him."

"And when was that?"

"That was . . . let's see . . . I reckon the last time I saw Ira was the day Grover and me went treasure hunting."

"Ira went with you, didn't he?"

"Yes, ma'am."

"And you haven't seen him since?"

"No, ma'am."

"You and he used to be pretty good friends, didn't you?"

"I reckon we did."

"But you're not anymore?"

"I didn't say that. I didn't say we weren't friends anymore. I just said I hadn't seen him since Grover and I took him treasure hunting with us."

"Mrs. McGruder told your father and me that you were the only person in town that Ira would talk to. What does he talk about?"

"Nothing. Missouri. He's got a goat and her name's Missouri. He talks to me about her sometimes."

"Has Ira ever said anything out of the way to you?"

"What do you mean?"

"Has he ever said anything wrong to you?"

"No. Ira's sweet. He wouldn't say anything wrong to anybody."

"Why are you sweating?"

"I'm not sweating."

"Yes you are. It's all over your face. Your face is covered with it."

"Well, I drink a lot of water and then I sweat. Why don't we go and eat now? I'm hungry, aren't you?"

"You're sweating because I'm questioning you about Ira. I want to know why, Ellen Grae, and if we have to sit here all night I'm going to find out."

"I'm not sweating because of Ira. I'm sweating because I'm hot."

"What did he say to you?"

"Nothing!"

"Are you sure?"

"Yes!"

Grace's own face was palely glistening. She leaned forward in her chair and spoke to me, slapping the words together, one by one. She said, "You talk about Ira in your sleep. Mrs. McGruder told us that she heard you talking about him in your sleep. Why?"

"I don't know why! I don't believe I do!"

"Mrs. McGruder wouldn't lie," Jeff said.

"I didn't say she lied! I just said . . . hell's afire, I don't know what I said!"

"Crying won't help," Jeff said. "And neither will swearing."

"I'm not crying! I'm not swearing! You're trying to twist me all up! You're trying to make me tell things about Ira that I don't want to tell!"

"What things about Ira don't you want to tell?"

"Nothing! I don't know anything about Ira I don't want to tell!"

"A minute ago you said you did. A minute ago you said we were trying to make you tell things about Ira that you didn't want to tell."

"Well you are! Leave me alone. Quit picking on me."

"We're not picking on you. We're just talking. Tell us about Ira."

"What do you want to know about him?"

"What does he talk to you about?"

"I told you. He talks to me about his goat. Her name's Missouri."

"What else?"

"Nothing! That's all!"

"Why is it you don't like to come to town anymore?"

"Because I just don't like to. Is there anything wrong with that?"

"No, there's nothing wrong with it but we think there's another reason. Is it because you're afraid you might run into Ira?"

"Of course not!"

"You're lying, Ellen Grae."

"I'm not! I'm not!"

"What things about Ira don't you want to tell?"

"Nothing! It's a secret! Nobody knows except me!"

"Knows what?"

"It wasn't his fault! They tried to kill him first! He told me that! It wasn't his fault! They were pulling him through the swamp . . . and they had a rattle-snake in a box . . . and they were poking at the snake with a stick . . . trying to make it bite Ira . . . but instead it bit them . . . and . . . and . . . he said . . . they both swelled up and died . . . and they were so far back in the swamp . . . and he didn't know what else to do . . . and he buried them!"

A silence followed during which Jeff wound his watch. I thought he was never going to stop.

A sigh came into Grace's face. She said, "Oh, honey."

"It's the truth! I'm not making it up!"

Jeff looked at Grace. "Well, this one stumps me. A guy who isn't all there in the brains department, who never says a word to anybody except our daughter, tells her that he buried his parents out in the swamp after a snake bit them, and she's made herself sick over it."

"They'll put him in jail or the crazy house," I whispered. "And he'll die and it'll be my fault."

Jeff's question traveled over my head to Grace. "What do you think we ought to do?"

"He trusts me," I said. "I'm the only one he ever talks to. I'm not making this up. The day we went treasure hunting . . . and we got to this place in the swamp . . . I know they're there . . . they've been there all the time . . . years and years . . . but it wasn't Ira's fault . . . he didn't kill them . . . the snake did."

Jeff said, "All right, Ellen Grae. All right. I think we've got it all now."

"What are you going to do?"

They shook their heads and said, "We don't know.

We'll do something but right now we don't know what."

I DIDN'T GO BACK to the McGruders' that night. After we ate some boxed fried chicken, which Grace sent out for, Jeff took a taxi and went out to the McGruders' and brought back some pajamas and other stuff for me.

I took a warm bath with some oil beads poured in the water.

We didn't talk any more about Ira.

About ten o'clock Jeff went to his room and Grace creamed her face and put on her pajamas and we went to bed.

No bedbugs bit us.

It stormed.

Early in the murky morning we rose and dressed and then Jeff came and we went to the drugstore for breakfast. While we were eating it Jeff talked about his work and Grace talked about her job. They both said they'd like to buy me a little present. "We thought maybe a ring like Rosemary's and a cute little gold wristwatch to match," they said. "Would you like that?"

My orange juice tasted like metal but I drank it anyway. "Thank you. That'd be nice."

Their smiles were easy and relaxed. "We forgot to ask you—how are things at school, Ellen Grae?"

"Fine. Just fine."

"No problems?"

"No. Mrs. McGruder helps me with my homework."

"What's your favorite subject this year?"

"English. I like words and stories."

Grace leaned and pulled a paper napkin from the metal holder on the table and fastidiously wiped her fingertips. "English was always my favorite subject too. And I just *loved* to write stories. What I created was always so real to me."

"Yes," I said, "what I create is always real to me too."

It was a delicious discovery. Grace hugged me.

Casually Jeff said, "How do you feel this morning?"

"Fine, thank you."

"Sleep all right?"

"Yes, sir. Did you?"

"Oh, I always sleep like a rock."

They were waiting for me. Their faces were bland but with little puddles of waiting in them. I said, "Looks like it's going to be a good day."

"Yes," they said. "It looks that way."

"We don't have to do anything, do we? We can just

spend all day enjoying ourselves, can't we? We're not worried about anything, are we?"

Grace said she wasn't sure and Jeff started talking to me about moral responsibility. "Those are two fearful words," he said. "And a little girl your age should not be too concerned with them and yet you must be. You realize that, don't you, Ellen Grae?"

I said, "I might realize it if I knew what they meant. Of course I know what morals are and I know what responsibility means. When you put them together I'm not exactly sure what they mean."

Jeff added sugar to his black coffee. "Moral responsibility is what you feel toward Ira. You feel that a moral wrong has been committed and because you have a conscience you are troubled and concerned and distressed. Because you know about this wrong you feel responsible."

"Jeff," I said, "I feel a lot better about things today than I did yesterday."

"Naturally. We're here now and you've confided in us and some of the weight has been lifted from you."

"So why don't we just skip it?"

"Is that what you want to do? Skip it?"

"It probably isn't true what he told me."

"Do *you* think it's true?"

"Anyway, even if it is true it wasn't his fault."

Jeff said, "Yes, all of us here understand that."

"It happened a long time ago. Maybe before I was even born. I don't know why *I* should have to worry about it."

"You don't have to. There's no law that says you have to."

I put a hunk of toast in my mouth, chewed it, and swallowed it. It went down dry. "You don't think they'd put Ira in the crazy house, do you, Jeff?"

"I don't know, Ellen Grae."

"Or in jail?"

"I don't know what they'd do to him, dear. I doubt very much if he'd go to prison. I don't know Ira—he's never said one word to me. When I buy peanuts from him I hand over the money and he hands over the sack and that's all. But offhand, just judging from what I've seen, I'd say he isn't mentally responsible."

"He isn't mentally responsible and so I'm morally responsible."

"You are only if you want to be, Ellen Grae. You let your conscience decide what's to be done."

"I have to decide all by myself?"

"Well, you're the one who's been worried about it. Grace and I haven't been. We didn't even know about it until yesterday."

"What would you do if you were me?"

"You know."

"I wish I was deaf," I said. "I wish he hadn't told me."

Jeff said, "Well, you aren't deaf and he *did* tell you. And now the question is, what are we going to do about it?"

"I don't see why I should be morally responsible for what somebody else has done."

"Your objection isn't an original one," Jeff said.

"Who would we have to go see?"

"The sheriff. Do you know him?"

"Only when I see him. His name's Irby Fudge. His office is right down the street."

Jeff bought me a pair of colored glasses before we left the drugstore. He said that they weren't to hide behind or cover up anything but that the sun looked like it was going to come out bright and hot and that I should get in the habit of wearing them, starting at once, to protect my eyes.

SHERIFF FUDGE HAD a plump, open face and a wide, friendly smile that said he liked you on sight, whoever you were and whatever your mission was. This smile of his invited you to like him also but in it was the hope that you hadn't come to him with any real trouble. His favorite word was shucks but before he let us know that he said he was mighty glad to meet us. Were we, he inquired, any relation to the Derryberrys over in Pierce County?

Jeff said no, no relation.

Sheriff Fudge said that that was too bad. That the Pierce County Derryberrys were mighty fine people. Law abiding and peace loving and minders of their own business. He invited us to sit down but there weren't enough chairs to go around so he sat on the corner of his desk. He said that he had seen me around town with Grover and the McGruders. What, he asked, could he do for us?

Jeff said, "Well, our daughter here is worried about one of your citizens. She's told us quite a story about him and now she wants to tell you."

"All right," said Sheriff Fudge and settled himself more solidly.

I told him my story about Ira. And all the time I was telling it it was plain to see that he considered all of it some kind of a sadly funny joke.

When I had finished with it and fell silent Sheriff Fudge smiled his broad smile, passed a hand over his short, burnished hair and said, "Shucks."

Jeff said, "I beg your pardon?"

"Shucks," Sheriff Fudge said grinning. " I beg *your* pardon, Mr. Derryberry, but if you could only know how silly your little girl's story sounds. Shucks.

Ira's parents aren't buried out in the swamp. They ran off and left him years ago. They're up north."

"Where up north?" Jeff asked.

Sheriff Fudge's expression gently apologized for his ignorance. He said, "Well now, shucks, I don't know that. That's something I can't tell you. But they're up there and you can rest assured of that."

Jeff reached inside his shirt cuff and his fingers found his watch. He wound it and wound it.

Sheriff Fudge slid from his desk leaving a round, polished spot. He walked around it to the window and looked out. Then he came back and sat down again. His smile was big and patient. He said, "Mr. Derryberry, has Ira ever talked to you about anything?"

Jeff stopped winding his watch. "Well, no. Of course I don't know him. I don't live here. I only come once in a while to visit my daughter."

Sheriff Fudge's smile grew. "It wouldn't make any difference if you *did* know him—if you *did* live here. You'd still never get him to talk to you. He doesn't talk to anybody. He just looks and points."

A dark rose blush crept into Jeff's cheeks. "Ellen Grae says that Ira talks to her."

Irby Fudge's laugh was rich and languid. "Yes, I know what Ellen Grae says. I know all about her stories. Everybody in Thicket does."

Grace removed her white gloves and reached into

her purse and withdrew a blue tissue but didn't use it for anything.

"My wife and I are friends with the McGruders," Sheriff Fudge explained. "We belong to the same church and my wife and Sally McGruder belong to the same bridge club."

"Mrs. McGruder is a wonderful person," Grace commented.

"They play every Wednesday night," Sheriff Fudge said. "Your little girl here provides the entertainment."

Jeff said, "What do you mean?"

"Story entertainment. Sally McGruder gets 'em from Ellen Grae and brings 'em to the bridge club and tells 'em. Then all the wives go home and the husbands hear 'em and everybody gets a good laugh. Don't you know about the stories your little girl tells?"

Jeff's face was stiff and embarrassed. "Yes, we know about them."

Grace put her gloves in her purse. She turned and looked at me.

I looked at Sheriff Fudge's plump leg with the shiny shoe on the end of it moving back and forth.

"Of course I wouldn't give you a nickel for a kid without imagination," Sheriff Fudge said in a kindly way.

I thought about Ira's mother and her husband. They must have been mean and ugly, big, wicked people with big, wicked thoughts and intentions.

Irby Fudge's foot looked comfortable in its soft, gleaming shoe. Above it the ankle was covered with an olive-colored sock, ribbed and very neat. I thought of Ira's feet which were shaped something like Grace's; high arched and free of corns because he hated shoes and wouldn't wear them even when it was cold. Ira didn't like noise either except natural ones, like the sound of the river sweeping past his shack and the sound of the wind, high in the mighty trees and the way the ground sounds underfoot on a still, frosty morning, full of sharp cracks and squeaks. Thicket had a noon whistle and once I had seen Ira cover his ears and shake during its wailing shriek.

"But sometimes their little imaginations run away with them," Sheriff Fudge said.

A picture of Ira's mother and her husband as they must have been came stealing into my mind. They would have had raw faces, sour and furtive, with sly eyes and mouths that had been desecrated by all the evil that lay within them. Anybody who could put a rattlesnake in a box and poke at it with a stick in the hopes that it would stick its vile head out and bite and bring death to somebody else had to look that way.

Sheriff Fudge was still swinging his foot and looking at me, and Grace was still turned around in her chair looking at me, and so was Jeff.

Jeff said, "Well, Ellen Grae?"

I thought, well I *did* try. Nobody can say that I didn't try. Hell's afire.

Grace said, "Ellen Grae?"

I said, "Well it's true that I do make up stories once in a while and sometimes they do kind of get away from me. Get bigger as I go along."

"Was that tale you told your father and me about Ira last night a story?" Grace asked.

I hung my head. "Sort of. I guess I got carried away with it."

Jeff's eyes brimmed with a sudden, deep sadness. He said, "Well, my word."

I pretended that my neck didn't have any muscles in it. That way it let my head hang loose against my chest. "I'm sorry. It's just that . . . when I think about stories and work them all out in my mind they get so real. I'm sorry. I don't want to cause anybody any trouble or hurt anybody. It's just that . . . well, it *was* real to me."

From Jeff's stomach there came a watery sound like it had just turned over.

Sheriff Fudge's foot, swinging back and forth, looked gay almost.

I raised my head and looked at them. Sheriff

Fudge's expression was amused, Jeff's was strained. Grace's lovely mouth was cool and so were her eyes. She said, "Oh, Ellen Grae, really. You disappoint me."

"I'm sorry," I whispered. "I'm really very sorry about the whole thing."

Sheriff Fudge's smile was luxuriant. It forgave me.

THEY WERE ANGRY. They went back to the Gingham Inn and packed up and went back to the city. I didn't get the promised watch and ring. Their good-bye kisses and hugs were not free and warm. They didn't look back and wave when their train pulled out of the station.

Mrs. McGruder was there and she put her arm around me and we stood there and watched until the last silver car, wriggling and swaying, had become a part of the misty distance. Then we walked back to where Mrs. McGruder had parked her car and got in it and drove around to the drugstore and each of us had a Black Cow which cost Mrs. McGruder a quarter apiece but she said she was feeling extravagant. She said she hoped I wouldn't vomit mine up because it had cream in it and would soothe my stomach.

I didn't vomit mine up.

We went home and Rosemary, her hair in curlers,

with egg white smoothed on her face to deal with sagging muscles and impending pimples, showed me her new wig which had arrived from the mail-order house that morning. She looked like a lion in it but I didn't say so. I told her that I thought the tawny tresses, so artfully arranged, bestowed a presence to her face.

"What do you mean presence?" she asked, drawing a purple bow on her mouth with a lipstick brush.

"Presence. Some people's faces have presence and some have absence. Yours has presence with that wig on. If I were you I'd wear it all the time. Who moved my books, Rosemary?"

"I did. Mrs. McGruder told me to clean up this room this morning. Your half was filthy. I found three pairs of dirty socks under your bed. Honestly, Ellen Grae."

"Rosemary, just for the experience you should spend a night at the Gingham Inn sometime."

"No thanks. That place gives me the creeps just to walk by it."

"They have bedbugs in their mattresses. Have you ever seen a bedbug?"

"Of course not."

"The Gingham Inn has thousands of them. You know those little buttons they put on mattresses to hold them together?"

"Yes, Ellen Grae."

"That's where they hide until you turn out the lights and go to sleep. Under those buttons."

"God, it was peaceful here without you around," Rosemary said. She erased the first purple bow and started on a second. "Excuse me, I forgot to ask you how your parents were."

"They're fine."

"Is your father still living in his garret?"

"Yes. He's going to move out about Christmas time though."

"To another garret, I suppose."

"No, not to another garret. He's decided to give up being an artist and go to Europe and become a *guérisseur*."

"What for?"

"Because *guérisseurs* make a lot of money and artists don't."

Inexpertly Rosemary removed the second mouth. Her efforts left a livid stain. Her cheekbones and forehead and temples, covered with dried egg white, had taken on a strange glow. She said, "I've got some stuff to dye my eybrows with but I suppose if I did it Mrs. McGruder would have a fit."

"He's going to live with this other very famous *guérisseur* on a houseboat in The Netherlands and take lessons from him."

"Cinnamon-colored eyebrows," Rosemary grieved,

leaning forward to examine the pale sepia question marks. "I hate them."

"All of the kings and queens in Europe go to him to get healed. A maharaja gave him a beautiful diamond crown one time just for curing him of a rare bone disease that had wasted away one of his legs up to the knee."

Rosemary examined her tongue. Its appearance, very pink and very shiny, obviously pleased her. She said, "I can't stand people with coated tongues. It makes me sick to my stomach. Your friend Grover was here about an hour ago. He said to tell you he was going down to his boat and that in case you came home any time soon for you to come on down. Honestly, Ellen Grae, your choice of friends is really disgusting."

Poor Rosemary.

Mrs. McGruder didn't jaw at me when I asked her if I could go down to the river and spend an hour or so with Grover. She made me two peanut butter and jelly sandwiches and two tuna fish salad ones and wrapped up a dozen ginger snaps in waxed paper. She did it lovingly and I told her I appreciated it and for some reason her eyes filled up with tears. She said, "Oh, Ellen Grae."

"Ma'am?"

"Nothing. I'm just glad your parents didn't take

you away from me. However trying you may be at times you still add something to my life."

"You add something to my life too, Mrs. Mc-Gruder. You and Mr. McGruder. Say, where *is* Mr. McGruder?"

"He's gone to the bakery for me."

"I love bakeries. They always smell so good. I used to know this girl whose father owned one and every afternoon after school we'd stop in at it and he'd give us stuff. For my birthday he gave me a cake that looked like a telegram. Yellow with black writing on it that said happy birthday. He was a dear man and everybody said that he didn't deserve the kind of fate that befell him. Even though he had a devil's temper and beat on his car with a two-by-four every time it wouldn't start."

"He *sounds* like his temper might have been a little unruly," Mrs. McGruder commented.

"Don't you want to know what his fate was?"

"Yes. Tell me about it."

"His car threw a rod one day while he was beating on it because it wouldn't start and it pierced his liver and he died."

"The rod pierced his liver?"

"It impaled him. I saw the whole thing. He looked so shocked when it happened. This rod, pointed on the end like an arrow, shot out like lightning from the hood. Right through the metal. And it impaled him. He was Catholic and the priest came right away and said the last rites for him. I gave him my linen handkerchief. I think Catholics die so pretty, don't you?"

Mrs. McGruder added two flowered paper napkins to the sack which contained the sandwiches and the ginger snaps. "I think," she said, "that for a little girl who is as much concerned with life as you are that you are much too occupied with death. Here is your lunch and Godspeed. Be back here by two o'clock at the latest."

THE DAY WAS AT its most glorious hour. Dressed in gold and blue light it sparkled. The face of the sky was wide and tranquil. The flat, brown land, faintly damp from its bath of the night before, looked revived. There were clusters of quiet clouds. It was hot and still. I heard the rush of the river long before I reached it.

Grover was sitting in the boat with his fishing hat pulled down low over his eyes. I threw my shoes and the lunch down at him but he didn't move. The boat rocked with my weight when I followed the lunch and the shoes and climbed aboard but all he did was let out a big sigh.

I said, "Hey, what're you doing?"

"Nothin'. Just sittin' here waitin' for you. Where've you been?"

"Nowhere. Hey, how come you aren't out with your uncle learning how to be a veterinarian today?"

"He gave me the day off. You want to go fishin'?"

"I reckon I do. You dug the worms already?"

"I dug a few. Somethin's been at my worm bed. I'm gonna have to put some chicken wire up around it I guess. Why don't you sit down?"

"I *am* sitting down. What do you reckon it was after your worms?"

"I dunno. A dog maybe."

"Dogs don't eat worms. Only birds and fish eat worms."

Grover pushed his hat to the back of his head. He looked at me. "Ellen Grae, I don't think I'm gonna be a veterinarian."

"You don't? What's wrong?"

"Well, you know that old sick cow I helped my uncle operate on last Saturday?"

"Yes."

"Somebody—I guess it was me—left a piece of towel in her. Yesterday the owner noticed the end of it stickin' out of the incision and called my uncle and my uncle had to go over there this morning and take it out."

"Oh, Grover, that's terrible. But you couldn't help it, could you?"

"Sure I could have but I didn't. I don't know how it happened except that I guess I was pretty excited. My first operation and all."

"Grover, it could have happened to anybody."

"No it couldn't have. It could only have happened to me. My uncle's right—I'm clumsy."

"I don't think you're clumsy. I think you're very graceful."

"Ellen Grae, I don't want to be graceful. I just don't want to be clumsy."

"Well, it's the same thing. If you're not clumsy you *have* to be graceful. That's the way the world is, Grover, and you might as well accept it."

"Okay, I'll accept it," Grover said, his face full of red irritation. He reached and pulled his oar from its lock. "If we're gonna go fishin' let's get goin'. Which way you want to go? Up the river or down?"

"Down will be all right. But I only want to go as far as the bend."

"I'll be lucky if that cow doesn't get gangrene," Grover muttered. He stood up, pulled his stomach in and then let it out again, removed his hat and then put it on again, sucked in his cheeks. "You can shove us off any time you get ready," he said, his eyes melancholy.

I shoved us off and we paddled out into the middle of the stream and headed downward. The river, chestnut-hued and spangled with patches of sun, received us smoothly. The wind was warm and courteous. Banners of gray moss swung without excitement from the trees on both banks. A bird's cry, loud and high but without alarm in it, pierced the air.

"Isn't it pretty out here?" I asked Grover. "See how pretty it is?"

He said, "Yeah, it's all right. I seen it before. Why are you rowin' so fast?"

"I'm not rowing fast. I'm just rowing. Do you want to stop and fish?"

"Naw, I don't think so. I don't feel like fishin' today."

"Grover," I said. "You'll feel better about things after a while. What you've got to do is put that cow out of your mind. When bad things happen to me that's what I do. I just put them out of my mind."

"How do you do that?"

"I just do it. Think about something else. That's what I do."

"Yeah," Grover said, hefting his paddle with new energy. "Yeah."

"You still know how to write poetry, Grover?"

"I dunno. I only wrote that one about the monk and I forgot how it goes."

"I'll bet if you tried to write another one you could. That'd take your mind off of the cow. Why don't you try it?"

"You mean now?"

"Sure. You're not doing anything else. Write a poem; it'll make you feel better."

"What about?"

"Grover, I don't know what to tell you to write about. Write about anything. Write about fish or birds or us out here having a good time."

"We're at the bend," Grover informed me. "You want to turn around and go back now?"

"In a minute. I just want to see if I can see Ira. Is that him out there hanging up clothes?"

Grover grinned for the first time that day. "No, that's Missouri. That's Ira over there by the trash pit eatin' paper."

I stood up in the boat and hollered and waved to Ira. With something white in his hand he turned from the line and waved back. Missouri lifted her head from whatever it was in the trash pile she was eating. Ira beckoned to her and she trotted over and stood beside him. He knelt and pointed to the boat and she leaned against him.

"You want to put in and visit him for a few minutes?" Grover asked.

"No. No, I just wanted to make sure he was all right. We can go on back now."

"Ira's nice," Grover remarked. "You're nice too, Ellen Grae. You always make me feel better about things."

His compliment uplifted me but kind of sorrowed

me too—brought a loneliness. For who was going to make *me* feel better about things? For just a second a pang of self-pity smote me but then I thought, Oh, hell's afire, Ellen Grae, you *wanted* to save Ira. Nobody made you. So quit your bellyaching. Maybe a way to make yourself feel better will come to you tomorrow, or the next day or the next. Something will come to you; it always does. Think positive.

I lifted my oar and helped Grover maneuver the boat around for the homeward journey.

Grover said, "You're a good sailor, Ellen Grae."

"Thank you, Grover. So are you."

We both laughed.

On the way back up the river, with me in the bow and Grover in the stern, Grover thought of a poem he could write to take his mind off the cow.

"It's about you," he said. And recited it to me:

ON THE RIVER AND AWAY FROM THE COW
AND ELLEN GRAE IS SITTIN' IN THE BOW.
WE'VE LEFT THE RIVER BEND BEHIND NOW.
SO LONG, IRA. GOOD-BYE, COW.